P9-CEO-193
PORTLAND, OR 97229
503-644-0043

Parent's Introduction

We Both Read books are specially designed to invite parents and children to share the reading of a story by taking turns reading aloud. This "shared reading" innovation, which was developed with reading education specialists, invites parents to read the left-hand pages. Children can then be encouraged to read the right-hand pages, which feature words and text specifically written for their level of ability. With books at five different reading levels, the *We Both Read* series is perfect for pre-readers, as well as beginning and reluctant readers!

Reading aloud is one of the most important activities parents can share with their child to assist them in their reading development. However, *We Both Read* books go beyond reading **to** a child and allow parents to share the reading **with** a child. As you read together, you will find the *We Both Read* books igniting interest in reading and accelerating reading development!

You may find it helpful to read the entire book aloud yourself the first time, then invite your child to participate in the second reading. We also encourage you to share and interact with your child as you read the book together.

If your child is having difficulty, you might want to mention a few things to help them. "Sounding out" is good, but it will not work with all words. They can pick up clues about the words they are reading from the story, the context of the sentence, or even the pictures. Some stories have rhyming patterns that might help. For beginning readers, you also might want to suggest touching the words with their finger as they read, so they can better connect the voice sound and the printed word.

Sharing the *We Both Read* books together will engage you and your child in an interactive adventure in reading! It is a fun and easy way to encourage and help your child to read—and a wonderful way to start them off on a lifetime of reading enjoyment!

WITHDRAWN
CEDAR MILL & BETHANY LIBRARIES

We Both Read: Lulu's Lost Shoes

Picture Book Edition

Reading Level (Child's Pages) – K to 1

Text Copyright ©2008, 2004 by Paula Blankenship
Illustrations Copyright ©2008, 2004 by Larry Reinhart
All rights reserved

We Both Read® is a trademark of Treasure Bay, Inc.

Published by Treasure Bay, Inc.
40 Sir Francis Drake Boulevard
San Anselmo, CA 94960

Printed in Malaysia

Library of Congress Catalog Card Number: 2007929914

ISBN-10: 1-60115-008-3
ISBN-13: 978-1-60115-008-0

We Both Read® **Books**
Patent No. 5,957,693

Visit us online at:
www.webothread.com

WE BOTH READ ®

Lulu's Lost Shoes

By Paula Blankenship

Illustrated by Larry Reinhart

TREASURE BAY

Morning shines in upon Lulu.
It shines on her little pet, Fred.
She wakes and she yawns and she stretches.
Then Lulu jumps up from . . .

. . . her bed.

Lulu heads down to the kitchen.
She flutters and flitters and dips.
She flies past her mom, who is cooking,
And into her chair . . .

. . . Lulu flips.

Mother says, "Lulu, stop playing.
Your breakfast is starting to cool!
And time's flying faster than you are.
Please hurry and head off . . .

. . . to school."

Nibbles and burps and "Excuse me!"
Then breakfast is finally done.
Her backpack and lunch are both waiting.
Now Lulu is ready . . .

. . . to run.

"Hold it!" calls Dad from his garden.
"Your feet are all wiggling free.
Go put on your shoes before leaving!
I saw them last night . . .

. . . by the tree."

Lulu looks under the willow.
Now where in the world could they be?
She asks her pet, Fred, "Have you seen them?"
He shrugs, saying, "Don't look . . .

. . . at me."

Lulu flies up to a beehive.
The bees may give Lulu some clues!
They're friendly and they can be helpful.
But they haven't seen . . .

. . . Lulu's shoes.

Lulu runs down to the water.
Her shoes may have dropped in the creek!
"Barrump," says a frog, "I can help you.
Just wait while I go take . . .

. . . a peek."

Frog tries his best, but can't find them.
There's nothing left here to discuss.
Poor Lulu's bare feet are still shoeless.
And here comes the big . . .

. . . yellow bus.

"Where are my shoes?!" Lulu wonders.
"I know they're not under the tree.
I know they're not up in the beehive.
My shoes must be hiding . . .

. . . from me!"

Up bumps the bus in the driveway.
The driver is given the news.
Then Mother Bug asks, "Can you wait here,
Until we can . . .

. . . find Lulu's shoes?"

Spiders and bugs are not patient,
Or quiet or sweet like a mouse.
They like to be flitting and flying!
And so they invade . . .

. . . Lulu's house!

Insects are helpful by nature.
They all want to help Lulu look.
They peer behind bookshelves and lampshades
To search every light bulb . . .

. . . and book.

Into the house leap the crickets.
The grasshoppers hop down the hall.
The spiders explore every bedroom.
The beetles have found . . .

. . . Lulu's ball.

Butterflies swing on the curtains.
The moths find a vacuum to use.
The stinkbugs explore every trash can.
But no one has found . . .

. . . Lulu's shoes.

Mother is not very happy.
Now EVERYONE here will be late!
And all of the shoes are still missing.
The only thing found . . .

. . . is a skate.

Lifting the couch is a termite,
A curious, strong little bug.
She carefully searches beneath it,
While others look . . .

. . . under the rug.

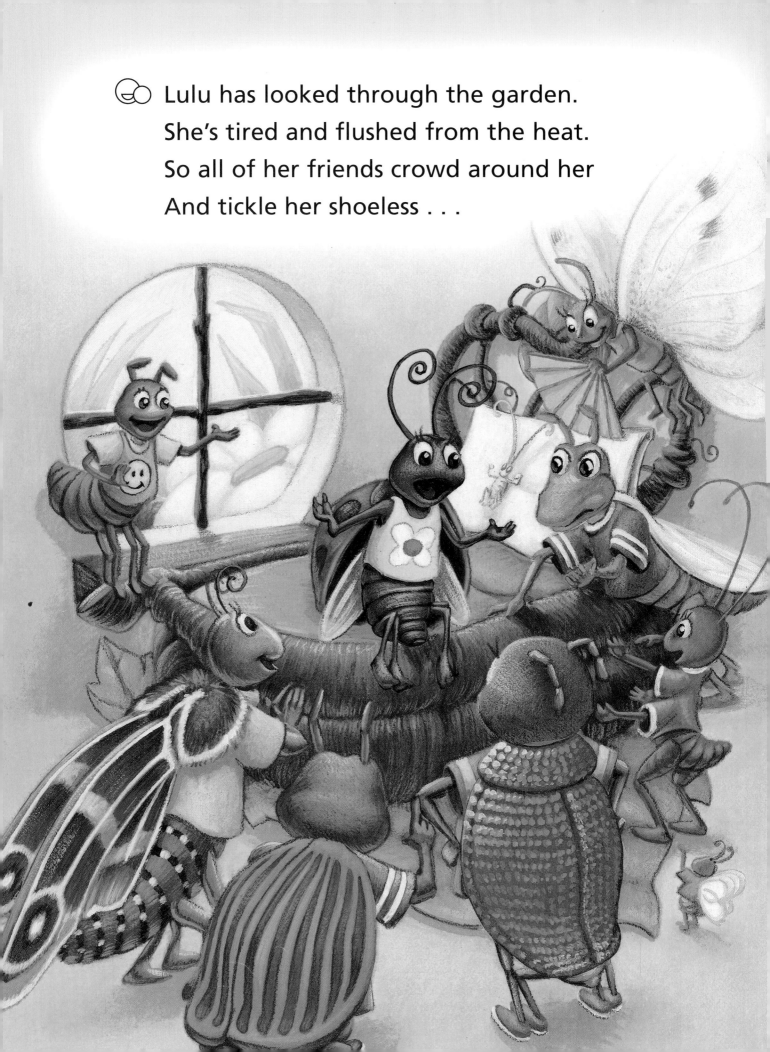

Lulu has looked through the garden.
She's tired and flushed from the heat.
So all of her friends crowd around her
And tickle her shoeless . . .

. . . bug feet.

Mother comes in and they tell her
They've searched every cranny and nook!
Then Mother says, "Peek in your closet.
It's always the last place . . .

. . . you look."

Suddenly, shoes fall around them.
They just can't believe the good news!
And everyone bursts out with laughter,
"At last we have found . . .

. . . Lulu's shoes."

If you liked *Lulu's Lost Shoes,* here is another
We Both Read picture book you are sure to enjoy!

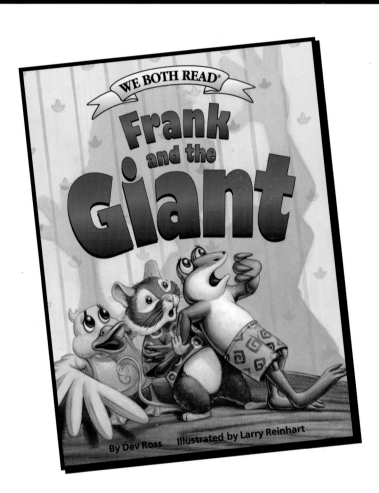

Frank, an adventurous little frog, is playing with
his friends, when suddenly his ball flies off and
bounces into the house of a giant! Frank's friends
are too scared to help him get his ball back, so he
sneaks into the huge house all by himself. There,
he is discovered by the giant, who seems big and
scary to Frank, but who is really just a friendly
little boy.

To see all the *We Both Read* books that are available,
including 40 titles available in paperback,
just go online to **www.webothread.com**